Flynn

Based on
The Railway Series
by the
Rev. W. Awdry

Illustrations by
Robin Davies

EGMONT

EGMONT
We bring stories to life

First published in Great Britain in 2016
by Egmont UK Limited
The Yellow Building, 1 Nicholas Road, London W11 4AN

Thomas the Tank Engine & Friends™

CREATED BY BRITT ALLCROFT
Based on the Railway Series by the Reverend W Awdry
© 2016 Gullane (Thomas) LLC. Thomas the Tank Engine & Friends and
Thomas & Friends are trademarks of Gullane (Thomas) Limited.
Thomas the Tank Engine & Friends and Design is Reg. U.S. Pat. & Tm. Off.
© 2016 HIT Entertainment Limited.

HiT entertainment

ISBN 978 1 4052 7984 0
62422/1
Printed in Italy

Written by Emily Stead. Designed by Claire Yeo.
Series designed by Martin Aggett.

FSC
MIX
Paper
FSC® C018306

Egmont is passionate about helping to preserve the world's remaining ancient forests.
We only use paper from legal and sustainable forest sources.

This book is made from paper certified by the Forestry Stewardship Council® (FSC®),
an organisation dedicated to promoting responsible management of forest resources.
For more information on the FSC, please visit www.fsc.org. To learn more about Egmont's
sustainable paper policy, please visit www.egmont.co.uk/ethical

This story is about Flynn,
Sodor's fastest fire engine! He can
travel on a track or go by road.
But one day Flynn forgot how to
use his road wheels! How would
he race to the rescue now?

Flynn was a fire engine with two sets of wheels. One set was for **riding** the rails and the other was for **rolling** on the roads.

One day, Victor was fixing Flynn's road wheels.

"Ready!" smiled Victor. "Now you can rescue by **road** or by **rail**."

But Flynn hadn't driven on roads for a long time. His wheels **wobbled** as he rumbled away.

Before long, Flynn stopped at a quiet junction.
He wanted to try his road wheels while no one
was watching.

He rolled slowly onto the road . . . but his wheels
wobbled and shook.

He didn't feel much like the famous **Fiery Flynn**!

Just then, Charlie chuffed by. "What's wrong?" he peeped. "You look like a **Big Red Wobble** on wheels!"

Flynn didn't want to look silly, so he rolled back onto the rails where his wheels wouldn't shake.

"The Sodor Search and Rescue team need your help," said Charlie. "**Hurry, hurry** . . . if you can!"

Rocky was glad when Flynn arrived at the Search and Rescue Centre. **"Emergency!"** roared Rocky. "The Fat Controller's shed is on fire!"

"Firefighter Flynn, **ready, steady** and **raring to go**!" Flynn called.

The quickest way to reach the shed was by road, but Flynn was worried about his wobbly wheels.

"I can get there faster than fast by rail!" he promised Rocky.

Riding the rails, Flynn felt fast and fearless. Then he saw Butch had broken down ahead.

"Can you give me a tow, Flynn?" called Butch.

Flynn wanted to help, but he knew that would mean using his wobbly road wheels. He didn't want to be called a **Big Red Wobble** again!

"Sorry, Butch," said Flynn. "I'm racing to an emergency." And he **rattled** away.

There was more trouble at the level crossing. Bertie had stopped – his engine had overheated!

"Please fetch some water to cool me down," **beeped** Bertie.

Flynn wanted to help, but he would have to go on the road. He didn't want Bertie's passengers to call him a **Big Red Wobble**.

"Sorry," called Flynn. "The Fat Controller's shed is on fire."

Flynn felt bad for not helping, but he didn't want his friends to see him **wobble** all over the roads. At last, he arrived at the burning shed.

"This is an emergency!" The Fat Controller said to Flynn crossly. "Why have you come by **rail**?"

Flynn didn't want to say that he was scared to go on the **road**. "I'm sorry, Sir," he cried.

"No excuses, Flynn," said The Fat Controller. "And no more delays."

Flynn looked at the fire. Then he looked at all the people watching him.

"They will call me a **Big Red Wobble**," he worried. "I can't go on the road. I just can't do it."

Flynn felt terrible. "I'm not Fiery Flynn, I'm Frightened Flynn. I can't save the shed and it's all my fault."

Suddenly a little boy shouted, "Our fire-fighting hero is here!"

"Hooray for Flynn!" everybody cheered.

Flynn looked and he listened . . . then his wheels stopped wobbling!

"I am Fiery Flynn! I want to be a hero! I don't mind being called a **Big Red Wobble** on wheels! I'm ready to rescue — here I come!"

Flynn raced onto the road. His wheels wobbled, but Flynn didn't mind! He was Firefighter Flynn of the Road **and** Rail!

"Stand back for Flynn!" The Fat Controller boomed.

Water whooshed into the flames. They **flickered** and **fizzled**, and soon the fire was out.

"Now I must hurry — I have others to rescue," Flynn said bravely.

First, Flynn fetched water to cool down Bertie's engine. Then he towed Butch safely home.

Thomas and Charlie were waiting to greet Flynn.

"Your wheels aren't wobbling," Charlie said. "You're not a **Big Red Wobble** any more!"

"No, you're a **Big Red Hero**!" Thomas smiled.

Flynn's wheels began to shake again. But this time it wasn't with worry — it was with joy!

More about Flynn

water cannon

ladder

lamp

axe

road wheel

railway wheel

Flynn's challenge to you

Look back through the pages of this book
and see if you can spot:

passengers

workmen

water cannon

burning shed

spanner

THE *THOMAS* ENGINE ADVENTURES

From Thomas to Harold the Helicopter, there is an Engine Adventure to thrill every Thomas fan.

  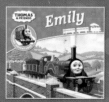